ALIENS STOLE MY UNDERPANTS 2

Poems chosen by Brian Moses

Illustrated by Lucy Maddison

MACMILLAN CHILDREN'S BOOKS

For Emma, Alyx and Penny – another intergalactic trio!

First published 2001
by Macmillan Children's Books
a division of Macmillan Publishers Ltd
25 Eccleston Place, London SW1W 9NF
Basingstoke and Oxford
www.macmillan.com

Associated companies throughout the world

ISBN 0 330 48346 3

1 3 5 7 9 8 6 4 2

A CIP catalogue record for this book is available from the British Library.

Printed by Mackays of Chatham plc, Chatham, Kent.

'Aliens on Vacation' from *Wish You Were Here (And I Wasn't)*. Text and illustration
© 1999 Colin McNaughton. Reproduced by permission of the publisher
Walker Books Ltd, London.
The poem 'The Alien Barbecues' by Brian Moses was especially written for
BBC Schools Online and features many of the 'favourite words' that children
e-mailed to the site.

ALIENS

Contents

ALIENS

ALIENS

Mistaken Identity

I thought I'd seen a monster
From Outer Outer Space,
'Til Dad said, 'No it's just your mum
With a mud-pack on her face . . .'

Clive Webster

Aliens Strike Again!

Aliens stole my underpants.
They stole my sister's blouses.
They stole my mother's knickers.
They stole my father's trousers.

Aliens stole my grandma's teeth.
They stole my grandpa's socks.
They stole the baby's nappies.
(Mum kept them in a box.)

Aliens stole my brother's glasses.
They stole my uncle's shirt.
They stole my best friend's baseball cap.
They stole Aunt Susan's skirt.

These wicked thefts by aliens
Have really got to stop.
I wonder why they do it?
Perhaps they have a shop?

John Kitching

An Alien
Shopping List

A solar-powered moon bike
An interstellar phone
An anti-matter sofa
For a crystal Martian home
A rocket-powered transporter
Irradiated shoes
Bioactive spectacles
Dehydrated stews
A supersonic spacesuit
An X-ray laser gun
Shopping for an alien
Is really lots of fun!

Ian Bland

Welcome

I came to the Entry Desk.
She didn't look up.
She was behind a screen.

Name? She barked.
Arfgam Banghwam, I said.
Planet of Origin?
Varglewark 3.
Colour?
Pinky-brown.
Not green?
Not green.
She didn't look up.

Appendages?
I'm sorry?
Legs, tentacles, tails etcetera.
Oh. Two arms, two legs.
She sighed.
Special antennae?
None.
Optical sensors?
Two eyes, brown.
Finally she looked up.

I'm sorry, you don't seem
Like an extra-terrestrial to me.
She looked disapproving, disbelieving.

I didn't want to disappoint her.
So I zapped her
With my third-brain zonic ray.
Bam!

She evaporated.
Satisfied? I asked.

Trevor Millum

NAME?

At the Bottom of the Garden

What's at the bottom of your garden?
A half-full sandpit covered in weeds;
A clump of dandelions spreading their seeds.

What's at the bottom of your garden?
A rusting bicycle against a wall;
A broken doll; an old football.

What's at the bottom of my garden?
An inter-galactic spacecraft refuelling station
Visited every night by faster than light machines
Cruising between the stars.
Of course, they put up their invisibility screens
Whenever I go near.

Well, it beats having fairies!

Alan Priestley

Supposed Encounter of the Alphabetical Kind

Alien Beings
Cunningly Descended Earthwards
From Galactic Holes,
In Jet-Kinetic-Laser
Masterships.

Not Offering Peace.

Quarrelsome Reptiles!

Savagely,
They Used Vaporising Weapons:

X – *Yonkers.*

ZAP ! ! !

Mike Jubb

My Dad Has Been Replaced

My dad
Has been replaced
By an alien.

He looks the same.
He sounds the same.
But he's not.

He has started
To do strange things:
The washing-up,
Making my pack-up,
Changing nappies.

And all this
Without being asked.

He gave me extra pocket money
And let me stay up late.
Was it a bribe
To keep me quiet?

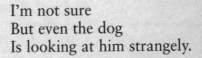

I'm not sure
But even the dog
Is looking at him strangely.

My dad
Has been replaced
By an alien.

So far only I know this.

Trevor Millum

'There's an Alien in the Shed . . .'

Andy Gibbons said
there was an alien
in his grandad's shed.

He said it was lime green
with bulging purple eyes –
the scariest thing he'd seen.

He said it had three feet
electric shocking hair
and ate raw meat.

He said he'd touched its head
and pulled away
long slimy threads.

He said I wouldn't
dare to look –
and so I said I would.

With shaking hands
I opened the shed door.
Inside were spiders' webs
        a buzzing wasp
        a dried-up bumble bee

but nothing alien-like
that I could see.

Tough luck!
said Andy, grinning.
Guess it's gone for tea.

Patricia Leighton

My Teenage Brother is from Another Planet

He moons around.
He stares into space.
Red spots erupt
all over his face.

He still likes football
but dreams about girls.
He now inhabits
an alien world.

That's it! He's an alien!
It's official. It's true.
He's been taken over.
But what can I do?

It's too late to save him
so the plan must be
to prevent the same thing
happening to me.

Bernard Young

Fan Letter to an
Alien Pop Sensation

Dear Stig Blurp,

I am thirteen eons old but I'm one of your biggest fans.
I have all your digital discs and interactive holograms.
You are the King of Spock and Roll, that's why I write
    this letter.
When I'm down I think of you and everything feels
    better.
You're the brightest star by far in our solar system
I've got three signed holographs and every day I've
    kissed them.
I love the way you cut your hair, especially on your
    chest.
Your song *'Baby Baby Grrrter Grax'* is the one I like
    the best.
At over eighteen kitos tall you really are so hunky
And with seven dancing feet your moonwalk is so
    funky.

I know you can't go everywhere when intergalactically
    famous
But next time you're on tour please come to Uranus.
I'd love to shake all your hands and kiss all those lips
My four knees turn to jelly when you swivel all your
    hips.
My hearts skip a beat or eight when you sing your song
Romantic lyrics dripping from your telescopic tongue . . .
'Zippult gortex tooger ooom unner pance eskree'
I sing them all the time and they mean all the world to
    me.
So send me something personal, please please write back
    soon.
You'll make this girl feel out of this world and over
    every moon.
Your appeal is universal so I know you'll understand
Just how much I love you.

Love from your greatest fan
X X Y X X X X Y

Paul Cookson

The ET Runway

*It is rumoured that in the Nevada Desert of America
there is a specially prepared ET Runway with welcome
messages permanently beamed into the sky to attract the
attention of low-flying extra-terrestrials. Meanwhile in a
back garden in Sussex . . .*

We've laid out what looks like a landing strip
in the hope of attracting an alien ship
and we've even managed to rig up a light
that will flash on and off throughout the night.
And we've spelt out 'welcome' in small white stones
and we've messed around with two mobile phones
till now they bleep almost continuously
and their signal plays havoc with next door's TV.
But it's for the greater good of mankind,
this could be a really important find.

And we're going to have an interstellar funday
when aliens land on *our* ET runway.
What a day it will be and what a surprise
when alien spacecraft snowflake the skies,
when strange beings christen our welcoming mat
to gasps of amazement, 'Just look at that!'
And to anyone out there listening in
the reception we'll give you is genuine:

We promise there'll be no limousines
to take you to tea with kings and queens.
No boring politicians from different lands,
no chatting on chat shows, or shaking of hands,
no scientists waiting to whisk you off

to investigate every bleep, grunt or cough.
It will only be us, just me and Pete
and a few friends from school you'll be happy to meet.
We could interview you for the school magazine:
'Do your spacecrafts run on gasolene?'

And we know it's not the desert in Nevada
but we really couldn't have tried much harder.
So if you can hear us, please make yourself known,
send us a signal, pick up the phone.
We've seen you out there, effortlessly gliding,
introduce yourselves now, it's time to stop hiding.

Brian Moses

Aliens on Vacation

They come from planets near and far,
Some big, some small, some quite bizarre.
Twinkle, twinkle, little star –
Aliens on vacation!

They've read the brochures, booked hotels,
Had their shots and said farewells.
Run for cover! Ring them bells!
Aliens on vacation!

Towards the Earth the pilot steers.
They've come to look for souvenirs,
Eat some pizza, drink some beers –
Aliens on vacation!

If you stare, they'll start a fight.
They sing rude songs and dance all night.
They go to bed when it gets light –
Aliens on vacation!

They hog the sunbeds round the pool,
Splash other guests and play the fool.
They write with spray-paint ALIENS RULE!
Aliens on vacation!

They plunder, photograph and scour.
Their spaceship has enormous power.
It takes on board the Eiffel Tower . . .
Aliens on vacation!

. . . From Israel, the Wailing Wall!
From London Town, the Albert Hall!
They take Mount Everest from Nepal . . .
Aliens on vacation!

      . . . Australia, they take Ayers Rock!
      From Scotland, they take Lomond Loch!
      From England, they take Big Ben's clock . . .
      Aliens on vacation!

 . . . From New York, the Empire State!
San Francisco, Golden Gate!
Never underestimate –
Aliens on vacation!

      With famous landmarks now just blanks,
      They check their oil and fill their tanks.
      They leave without a word of thanks –
      Aliens on vacation!

And as they leave, the aliens cheer
And chuck out empty cans of beer;
'We'll all be back again next year!' –
Aliens on vacation!

      There's just one thing they overlook:
      That when, next year, they try to book,
      The phone just might be off the hook –
      To aliens on vacation!

Colin McNaughton

Double Yellow Trouble

Our town lies in smouldering ruins –
just rubble and flickering fires.
And who is to blame?
Well, I'll tell you his name.
It's that new traffic warden called Squires.

You can't blame an alien for parking
on bright yellow lines painted double.
In Space, all the scout ships,
and small runabout ships,
can park where they like without trouble.

But Squires lost his cool in the High Street;
a UFO had parked rather careless.
He wrote out a ticket,
and then tried to stick it
on this bug-eyed creature, all hairless.

This upset the purple-skinned alien.
He puffed out a cloud of thick smoke.
And then came disaster –
he whipped out his blaster,
and flattened the town at a stroke!

Beware, then, of badly parked UFOs,
with bright flashing lights, gently humming.
Don't stop and deplore them.
Pass by and ignore them . . .
and hope Warden Squires isn't coming.

Barry Buckingham

Stop, Thief!

When we went to the cinema
to see the latest space movie
  we didn't expect a spacecraft
    to roar off the screen,
      brake sharply
        and hover over us
          as we cowered in our seats.

We didn't expect the spacecraft door
to flip open in a flash
  so that glaring lights
    blazed into our eyes
      and blinded us
        temporarily.

And we didn't expect
that whiplash tentacles
  would crack down,
    encircle our tubs of popcorn
      and whisk them up through
        the quickly closing door
          while crackles of weird alien laughter
            burst from the cinema loudspeakers.

And after all that,
we certainly didn't expect the spacecraft
   to cruise back onto the screen again
     and resume its part in the movie
       leaving us sitting open-mouthed
         with rumbling stomachs
           and eyes popping in
             astonishment.

Penny Kent

I Come in Peace

The Alien stepped forwards,
It held its flippers high,
'I come in peace,' it whistled,
'From somewhere in the sky.'

The Earthling made no answer,
So the Alien tried again,
'Please take me to your leader –
I think my meaning's plain.'

No smiles disturbed the stillness
Of the Earthling's frosty face.
'Behold!' the Alien gurgled,
'I bring you gifts from Space.'

At last, when all its efforts
Had failed, and failed some more,
The Alien flew homewards
To its friendly, Alien shore.

But far away, its presents
Lay squashed between two cars,
While a rather puzzled petrol pump
Gazed blankly at the stars.

Clare Bevan

Parlez-Vous Zork?

When our visitor from Zork arrived
I couldn't make out a word it said.
Nor could Mum.
But our baby could.

They got chatting straight away
And never stopped.
All day long it was,
MOOZLEWOB, DURDLE-DURDLE, PTHHHHH,
And stuff like that.
Such earnest conversations.

I hope when our baby learns English
He'll be able to remember,
And will tell me
What they were about.

Frances Nagle

Snack Attack

We're
aliens, we're
coming, through
interstellar space, racing
meteors and comets at a hyper-warp-speed pace.
Our latest information leads to Earth – our destination.
Just as soon as we arrive, the freshest food – we'll eat it *live*.
Crunchy, chewy and nutritious –
we're told Earthlings are
DELICIOUS!

Liz Brownlee

Invasion

When the aliens landed on earth
their mighty battle fleet
spread out in formation
along the shoreline of a sea.

When the aliens landed on earth
their commander stood on the shore
and claimed the planet. After all,
there was no resistance to their force.

When the aliens landed on earth
a boy, stepping over a puddle,
squashed them all.

Dave Calder

Trouble on the Spaceway

We started out from Neptune,
At helter-skelter speed,
For a Martian celebration,
On the planet Gannymede.

But we didn't know the misery,
That we were going to meet,
As we passed the thunder-buses,
And a flash new Venus jeep.

There were space-works on the orbital,
The traffic pulse was down,
A hold-up on the Pluto route,
And worm holes spinning round.

The weather was atrocious,
Solar storms and rainbow dust,
And the supernova Rover
Was growling fit to bust.

By the time we passed old Ceres,
Hurling rocks with all his might,
The craters in our camper-van
Were not a pretty sight.

We took the path to Jupiter,
A tried and tested rule,
But the camper-van began to squeal,
I'm running out of gruel!

So we left the super spaceway,
And took the autobahn,
And through the laws of retro-time,
Arrived where we began.

Mary Green

The Alien Barbecues

A heavenly pong that we just couldn't trace
has been drifting around up here in space,
till our saucers returned with wonderful news –
it's the smoke from your back garden barbecues.

They smell saucy, spicy and appetising,
scrumptious and luscious, quite tantalising,
delightful, delectable, delicious, it's true,
succulently savoury, nutritious too.

Now we've been sent to discover more
of this fast food formula that we can't ignore;
for we've cooked it ourselves and we can't get it right
and that's why we keep calling round every night.

It's so munchable, crunchable, truly scrummy,
gorgeous, mouth-watering, chewy and yummy.
It tickles our tastebuds, our tongues become tangled
but it still isn't right and our teeth have got mangled.

You see all we have fed on for many light years
are red planet slugs kebabbed on small spears
like the party sausage you eat from a stick
but we're telling you now, they're making us sick.

They're slimy, they're yucky, disgustingly green
the most revolting creatures we've ever seen.
They're stinky and vile with a vinegary taste,
gungey and gooey like smelly fish paste.

So please help us out, we're really uptight.
Tell us the secret, we'll get out of your sight.
We won't invade, we'll turn round and go
once you've told us all that we need to know.

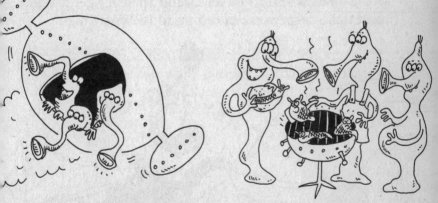

And when we're quite sure that we've got it right
we'll invite you to Mars for a fantastic night.
Red planet slugs you just won't refuse
when they're grilled on our alien barbecues.

Brian Moses

Life in Alien Nation

Alien and Alienesse
Have a beautiful alienome,
Where they live with their alienildren
And their bright red aliengnome.

He is an alienologist
At the alienfirmary,
Finding cures for alienitis
In the local community.

Alienache is common,
Alienella is rare
But is spread by disease in alien eggs,
So owners take note – and BEWARE!

She is an alienobat,
Every morning she swings and she climbs.
Then after lunch she's an alienmum
Reading alienursery rhymes.

They speak in Alienanish,
They travel by alienar,
Their life in Alien Nation
Is alieneally bizarre!

Daphne Kitching

Alien Invasion

Zigblad The Great, Mighty Warlord of the planet Drob,
Grand King and High Emperor of the Fifteen Galaxies,
Dragon Slayer, Beast Killer, Destroyer of Monsters
landed firmly on the planet's surface, flourished
his Vorgle Blast Super Ray Gun that once smashed the
   dreaded Smigz,
the Mighty Sword of Trygarth which slew the Seven
   Headed Spangleglurk,
the Shield of Vambloot which protected him from harm,
the Ring of Skigniblick, which gave him all power
and standing fast the mighty warrior
spoke out loudly, his voice ringing like the Great Bell
   of Hootrim,
I claim this planet and all its creatures for the Empire
   of Drob.
Have great fear of me and my warriors, tremble at our
   mighty voices.

Unfortunately,
he was suddenly swallowed
by a passing magpie, who thought he was
a very juicy beetle.

David Harmer

There's a Black Hole in the Corner of My Bedroom

So far I have lost
six red pencils, sixteen football stickers,
a million paper clips,
twenty-seven toffees coated with fluff,
a balloon, nine biros, some bubble gum
and twelve marbles.

Last week
I lifted the carpet at the corner
and saw a swirling tunnel of blackness
wobbling into nothing.
I pushed away the clouds with a pencil
and there was a little planet
twirling like a tiny ball.

Now they visit me. They fly
red and blue pointed spaceships
covered in dazzling tiny wires.
They talk to me and say,
Thank you for the toffee-flavoured fluff –
we love all your presents.

But they are puzzled by the marbles.
They never saw them. Perhaps
there is another black hole
inside my black hole
with another planet under that one
and so on forever.

My dad says there's a black hole
in his pocket every time we go shopping.
My mum says
I should be more careful with my things,
not keep losing them,
but you and I know different,
don't we?

David Harmer

Ring of Truth

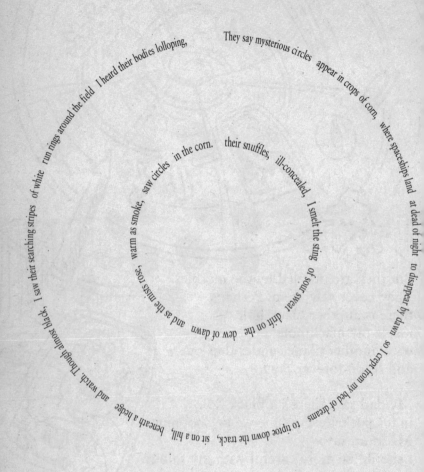

They say mysterious circles appear in crops of corn, where spaceships land at dead of night to disappear by dawn so I crept from my bed of dreams to tiptoe down the track, sit on a hill, beneath a hedge and watch. Though almost black, I saw their searching stripes of white run rings around the field I heard their bodies lolloping,

saw circles in the corn. their snuffles, ill-concealed, I smelt the sting of sour sweat drift on the dew of dawn and as the mists rose, warm as smoke,

Gina Douthwaite

The People Next Door

There are new people living next door,
They're as quiet as a comatose mouse,
We wouldn't have known there was anyone there,
But a blue light came on in the house.

And sometimes when they think no one's about,
A small head peeks out through the door,
But we never see any adult over there,
They all seem not much older than four.

Our dog used to chase rabbits in the garden next door,
But he hasn't gone near since they came,
The ducks in the pond flew away it seems,
And that's a pity, they were getting so tame.

And the rabbits that were always hopping next door
In their dozens have all disappeared,
In their garden, there isn't a bird or a bee,
Though we've got plenty, isn't that weird?

The vicar went over to welcome them in,
And now he is acting so odd!
If you ask him their names, or what they are like,
He'll just cross himself twice, smile and nod.

The postman who used to deliver their mail
Has gone away, no one knows where,
And that's such a shame because if anyone could
He would tell us what they're like over there.

The social worker went round to find out
Why the children weren't at school,
But we haven't seen her since, so I guess
She's probably visiting her mum in Blackpool.

Then we got a letter, pushed through the door.
Written on paper that just seems to glow,
Inviting us over for supper and games
Tonight at six. Do you think we should go?

Valerie Bloom

Alien Abduction

My brother claims that aliens
Abducted him last night
They beamed him straight up from his bed
Into their disc of light.

He says the 'things' that took him
Had bulbous heads of blue
And X-ray eyes that glowed bright red
When looking into you.

They had six scaly fingers,
Four legs and sixteen toes
He reckons they had silver teeth
Below a trumpet nose.

They carried out all kinds of tests
They measured height and girth
They used all sorts of instruments
We've never seen on Earth.

They looked into his stomach with
A type of 'space age' dart
They pulled out hair, they scraped off skin
Then analysed his heart.

He says he never felt a thing
Throughout he stayed quite calm
Even when they probed his head
And took apart his arm.

He says that when they'd finished
They showed him round their ship
Then beamed him straight back to bed
To carry on his kip.

I don't dismiss this story
It's possible I s'pose
Of course he'll never prove it
But then again who knows.

But if they came to study us
One question still remains
Why on Earth choose Trevor
And not someone with brains?

Richard Caley

Ship Shape Space Ship

Ship shot at by droids?
Been sucked into voids?
Or did space sickness strike all your crew?
If you're cratered by comets
And submerged in vomit
Let us make your ship shipshape for you.

We'll clean out your spark plugs
And vaporise space bugs,
Check your warp drive is faster than lightning.
We repair dents and holes
And replace toilet rolls
Because Outer Space can be frightening.

Alien ships huge or tiny
Will be shipshape and shiny.
Everyone's spreading the word –
If you want the best
Call S.S.S.S.
Our service is out of your world!

Jane Clarke

Alien Celebration Song

Usually sung with a great waving of tentacles.

Uhrghl pffflli nnng fu
Uhrghl pffflli nnng fu
Uhrghl pffflli zurrrrrrrghhh tzzzzt grrrk –
Uhrghl pffflli nnng fu!

Penny Dolan

Alien Invaders

The space invaders slowed their ship,
and, weapons held in vice-like grip,
entered shuttles. Earthbound, they
landed on a rainy day
outside a little English town.
Ferocious aliens, green and brown
with small red eyes and sabre claws,
sharp fangs and slavering, drooling jaws
leapt, yelling into driving rain
and were washed, still yelling, down a drain.
They were but one centimetre high
so no one heard their angry cries.
Puddles formed. As people waded,
no one knew they'd been invaded.

Marian Swinger

An Alien Limerick

As on Red Planet, Mars, we alighted,
A very large banner we sighted.
'That's the answer,' I said,
'To why Mars is called "red"'.
It said MARTIANS ALL LOVE MAN UNITED.

Eric Finney

Crop Circles

It's a common belief that crop circles
are attempts by visitors from Space
to establish communications
with us of the Human Race.

But don't be fooled by the 'experts'
who think they know better than me.
Crop circles are done by UFO yobs . . .

It's alien graffiti, see?

Barry Buckingham

From Another Planet

When you first came,
we laughed at you
and called you sassenach.
As if you were from another planet.

Maggy Stewart pinched your Penguin.
Dougy McLean made jokes,
like 'Did you come intruder window?'
As if you didn't belong.

Mary McQueen pulled your plaits,
Jamie Souness called them ears,
and asked if they were your antennae.
As if you were a weirdo from outer space.

Hamish Bruce mocked your English accent,
Angus Dixon wouldn't stand behind you in the line.
Jean McLeod asked you for Mars Bars.
As if you were from Mars.

It was when we saw you standing by the radiator,
   crying, and
holding something in your hand, and
we knew that you had found Honey the Hamster, and
you said you wouldn't let her go until
we all stopped teasing and bullying you and
Jamie Souness was the first to say he was sorry and
Dougy McLean cried too because
he was the one who had left the cage open and
he was going to have to tell Mr Spink the headmaster
   that

it was his fault but he just said oh my god, and
you handed me Honey the Hamster because
it was my turn to feed her;

it was then that I really saw you
for the first time.

Judy Tweddle

A selected list of poetry books available from Macmillan

The prices shown below are correct at the time of going to press. However, Macmillan Publishers reserve the right to show new retail prices on covers which may differ from those previously advertised.

The Secret Lives of Teachers   0 330 34265 7
   Revealing rhymes, chosen by Brian Moses   £3.50

Aliens Stole My Underpants   0 330 34995 3
   And other intergalactic poems, chosen by Brian Moses   £2.99

Parent-Free Zone   0 330 34554 0
   Poems about parents, chosen by Brian Moses   £2.99

Don't Look at Me in That Tone of Voice   0 330 35337 3
   Poems by Brian Moses   £2.99

Barking Back at Dogs   0 330 48009 X
   Poems by Brian Moses   £2.99

Welcome to the Snake Hotel   0 330 48261 0
   Poems chosen by Brian Moses   £3.50

The Penguin in the Fridge   0 330 48019 7
   And other cool poems by Peter Dixon   £3.50

All Macmillan titles can be ordered at your locasl bookshop or are available by post from:

Book Service by Post
PO Box 29, Douglas, Isle of Man IM99 1BQ

Credit cards accepted. For details:
Telephone: 01624 675137
Fax: 01624 670923
E-mail: bookshop@enterprise.net

Free Postage and Packing in the UK.
Overseas customers: add £1 per book (paperback)
and £3 per book (hardback).